# Tamerlane

*Edgar Allan Poe*

Tamerlane by Edgar Allan Poe
First Published: 1827
Cover Image: Portrait of Edgar Allan Poe
Artist: Oscar Halling
Date: 1848
License: CC0 1.0 Universal (CC0 1.0)

Published by Digibooks OOD / Demetra Publishing, Bulgaria.



Contact: info@demetrapublishing.com

ISBN: 9781091653764

# CONTENTS

# PREFACE BY THE EDITOR

THE SAME YEAR that witnessed the publication, at Louth in Lincolnshire, of Alfred Tennyson's first schoolboy volume of verse also gave birth, at that literary capital of the United States of America which takes its name from another Lincolnshire town, to Edgar Poe's maiden book. Unlike the sumptuous and elegant "Poems by Two Brothers," however, which the adventurous publishers actually had the temerity to issue in large-paper form as well as in the ordinary size, Edgar Poe's volume (if it can be dignified with that designation) is the tiniest of tomes, numbering, inclusive of title and half-titles, only forty pages, and measuring 6⅜ by 4⅛ inches. Its diminutiveness, probably quite as much as the fact that it was "suppressed through circumstances of a private nature," accounts for its almost entire disappearance. The motto on the title-page purports to be from Cowper: that from Martial, which closes the Preface (*Nos hæc novimus esse nihil*), was, by a curious coincidence, the very same that figured on the title-page of Alfred and Charles Tennyson's Louth volume.

In 1827, when the little "Tamerlane" booklet was thus modestly ushered into the world, Poe had not yet attained his nineteenth year. Both in promise and in actual performance, it may claim to rank as the most remarkable production that any English-speaking and English-writing poet of this century has published in his teens.

In this earliest form of it the poem which gives its chief title to the little volume is divided into seventeen sections, of irregular length, containing a total of 406 lines. "Tamerlane" was afterwards remodelled and rewritten, from beginning to end, and in its final form, as it appeared in the author's

edition of 1845, is divided into twenty-three sections, containing a total of 243 lines. Eleven explanatory prose notes are added, which disappear in all subsequent editions. A critic whose familiar acquaintance with the text of Poe gives weight to his verdict, declares that although "different in structure, and explaining some things which, in later copies, are left to the imagination, the Tamerlane of 1827 is in many parts quite equal to the present poem."

Of the nine "Fugitive Pieces" which follow only three, and these in a somewhat altered form, were included by the author in his later collection. The remaining six have never been reprinted in book form, although they were, together with a few extracts from the earliest version of "Tamerlane," printed (so incorrectly, however, as to be practically valueless,) in a magazine article on "The Unknown Poetry of Edgar Poe," contributed by Mr. John H. Ingram to *Belgravia* for June 1876.

I have no desire to disparage or underrate, and have already taken occasion to render tribute to, the worthy and loyal service and labour of love performed by Mr. Ingram, with zeal if not always with discretion, on the text of Poe, and still more notably in clearing his life and memory from the aspersions of contemporary calumniators. But, in justice both to myself and to others, I am compelled to repudiate and refute the untenable and, as it seems to me, preposterous claim recently put forward by him in the columns of a leading literary journal, to be the discoverer of the first edition of Poe's *Tamerlane*, and to possess a sort of moral right of monopoly over it.

The facts are simply these, and had I been allowed, as in all fairness I ought to have been, to disclose them in the columns of the journal which gave insertion to Mr. Ingram's *ex parte* statement, I need not have troubled the reader with them here. First as to discovery. The only copy of Edgar Poe's 1827 volume at present known to have escaped destruction, came into the possession of the British Museum on the 10th October 1867, which date is (according to custom) officially impressed in red, at the end of the volume, *i.e.*, at the bottom of page 40, under the last note. I believe I am correct in stating that Mr. Ingram did not commence his work on the text of Poe until several years after this: it was certainly not until nearly nine years after that he communicated to the public his account of the "Tamerlane" volume, with extracts, first to *Belgravia* for June, 1876, and afterwards to the *Athenæum* for July 29, 1876. The extracts in the *Athenæum* were limited to four lines of verse, and an imperfect transcript of the title; but the paper in *Belgravia* contained copious extracts from the longer poem of "Tamerlane," and of the nine "fugitive pieces," the six suppressed ones were given *in extenso*. In the "Tamerlane" extracts, as thus printed by Mr. Ingram, there were two textual misprints in the Preface, and five in the text; in the "Fugitive Pieces" there were at least five misprints, seriously affecting the sense. This assertion can easily be proved and cannot possibly be refuted. And now as to the claim to monopoly. Since the publication of his *Belgravian* article, shown to be valueless on account of its inaccuracy, nearly eight more years have elapsed, and until the announcement of the present venture, Mr. Ingram had made no attempt, and given no sign of his intention, to reissue the contents of Poe's 1827 booklet, either separately or in any other shape. His claim to monopoly, therefore, is just as unreasonable and absurd as I have already proved his claim to discovery to be.

"There are several palpable *errata*," as Mr. Ingram has remarked, "in Edgar Poe's first book" (and which therefore all the more should have had no fresh ones superadded). These I have thought it best to correct, wherever they are perfectly obvious (a list of them and of proposed conjectural emendations is appended), and I have also reduced the orthography and punctuation to a uniform standard. The present case was not one where a facsimile reprint was desirable, — the typography, arrangement, size, and general appearance of the original edition being unsatisfactory in the extreme.

Should this attempt to perpetuate and preserve from destruction a little volume to which might hitherto have been applied the French bibliographer's epithet of "introuvable," prove acceptable to admirers and lovers of Poe, I hope eventually to have the opportunely of reissuing successively the hardly less rare volumes published by him at Baltimore in 1829 and at New York in 1831.

Richard Herne Shepherd.

P.S. — Mr. George Edward Woodberry, of Beverly, Mass., the author of an excellent "History of Wood-Engraving," who is preparing a biography of Poe for the series of "American Men of Letters," now publishing by Messrs. Houghton and Co., of Boston, writes to me (under date Jan. 1, 1884) as follows: —

"Of the original edition Mr. Ingram states that he has a copy, and thinks it unique because Poe stated that the edition was suppressed. I do not think it was suppressed, however, and as you may be interested in the matter I extend this note. The printer, Mr. Calvin F. S. Thomas, was a very obscure man, who had a printer's shop at Boston only in that year; I have sought through all the Thomas families of Mass., Maine, Rhode Island, Maryland, Ohio, etc., to which he was likely to belong, and there is no trace of him. I can find no other book with his imprint. Consequently I suppose the edition to have been small and obscure. It was published between June and October, 1827, probably in June. It was not noticed or advertised, apparently, but it occurs in the *North American Review*'s quarterly list of new publications, in the October number, 1827 [vol. xxv. p. 471]. How Poe, a youth of eighteen, in a strange city, friendless and penniless as he was, persuaded this unknown printer to issue his volume, is a mystery to me. I have talked with old men, and had the printers and publishers who survive from that time interrogated, but though Boston was a small town, no one knew Thomas or ever heard of him. You may be sure, however, that the Mr. Ingram who seems to own Poe, is wrong in believing that the volume was only printed, and not published. Poe left Boston in October of that year."

# AUTHOR'S PREFACE

THE GREATER PART of the Poems which compose this little volume were written in the year 1821-2, when the author had not completed his fourteenth year. They were of course not intended for publication; why they are now published concerns no one but himself. Of the smaller pieces very little need be said: they perhaps savour too much of egotism; but they were written by one too young to have any knowledge of the world but from his own breast.

In "Tamerlane" he has endeavoured to expose the folly of even *risking* the best feelings of the heart at the shrine of Ambition. He is conscious that in this there are many faults (besides that of the general character of the poem), which he flatters himself he could, with little trouble, have corrected, but unlike many of his predecessors, has been too fond of his early productions to amend them in his *old age.*

He will not say that he is indifferent as to the success of these Poems — it might stimulate him to other attempts — but he can safely assert that failure will not at all influence him in a resolution already adopted. This is challenging criticism — let it be so. *Nos hæc novimus esse nihil.*

# TAMERLANE

## I.

I HAVE sent for thee, holy friar;
But 'twas not with the drunken hope,
Which is but agony of desire
To shun the fate, with which to cope
Is more than crime may dare to dream,
That I have call'd thee at this hour:
Such, father, is not my theme —
Nor am I mad, to deem that power
Of earth may shrive me of the sin
Unearthly pride hath revelled in —
I would not call thee fool, old man.
But hope is not a gift of thine;
If I *can* hope (O God! I can)
It falls from an eternal shrine.

## II.

The gay wall of this gaudy tower
Grows dim around me — death is near.
I had not thought, until this hour

When passing from the earth, that ear
Of any, were it not the shade
Of one whom in life I made
All mystery but a simple name,
Might know the secret of a spirit
Bow'd down in sorrow, and in shame. —
Shame, said'st thou?
    Ay, I did inherit
That hated portion, with the fame,
The worldly glory, which has shown
A demon-light around my throne,
Scorching my sear'd heart with a pain
Not Hell shall make me fear again.

## III.

    I have not always been as now —
The fever'd diadem on my brow
I claim'd and won usurpingly —
Ay — the same heritage hath given
Rome to the Cæsar — this to me;
The heirdom of a kingly mind —
And a proud spirit, which hath striven
Triumphantly with human kind.
    In mountain air I first drew life;
The mists of the Taglay have shed
Nightly their dews on my young head;
And my brain drank their venom then,
When after day of perilous strife
With chamois, I would seize his den

And slumber, in my pride of power,
The infant monarch of the hour —
For, with the mountain dew by night,
My soul imbibed unhallow'd feeling;
And I would feel its essence stealing
In dreams upon me — while the light
Flashing from cloud that hover'd o'er,
Would seem to my half closing eye
The pageantry of monarchy!
And the deep thunder's echoing roar
Came hurriedly upon me, telling
Of war, and tumult, where my voice,
My *own* voice, silly child! was swelling
(O how would my wild heart rejoice
And leap within me at the cry)
The battle cry of victory!

*****

## IV.

The rain came down upon my head
But barely shelter'd — and the wind
Pass'd quickly o'er me — but my mind
Was maddening — for 'twas man that shed
Laurels upon me — and the rush,
The torrent of the chilly air
Gurgled in my pleased ear the crush
Of empires, with the captive's prayer,
The hum of suitors, the mix'd tone
Of flattery round a sovereign's throne.

The storm had ceased — and I awoke —
Its spirit cradled me to sleep,
And as it pass'd me by, there broke
Strange light upon me, tho' it were
My soul in mystery to steep:
For I was not as I had been;
The child of Nature, without care,
Or thought, save of the passing scene. —

## V.

My passions, from that hapless hour,
Usurp'd a tyranny, which men
Have deem'd, since I have reach'd to power,
My innate nature — be it so:
But, father, there lived one who, then —
Then, in my boyhood, when their fire
Burn'd with a still intenser glow;
(For passion must with youth expire)
Even *then*, who deem'd this iron heart
In woman's weakness had a part.
I have no words, alas! to tell
The loveliness of loving well!
Nor would I dare attempt to trace
The breathing beauty of a face,
Which even to *my* impassion'd mind,
Leaves not its memory behind.
In spring of life have ye ne'er dwelt
Some object of delight upon,
With steadfast eye, till ye have felt

The earth reel — and the vision gone?
And I have held to memory's eye
One object — and but one — until
Its very form hath pass'd me by,
But left its influence with me stilL

## VI.

'Tis not to thee that I should name —
Thou canst not — wouldst not dare to think
The magic empire of a flame
Which even upon this perilous brink
Hath fix'd my soul, tho' unforgiven,
By what it lost for passion — Heaven.
I loved — and O, how tenderly!
Yes! she [was] worthy of all love!
Such as in infancy was mine,
Tho' then its *passion* could not be:
'Twas such as angel minds above
Might envy — her young heart the shrine
On which my every hope and thought
Were incense — then a goodly gift —
For they were childish, without sin,
Pure as her young example taught;
Why did I leave it and adrift,
Trust to the fickle star within?

## VII.

We grew in age and love together,
Roaming the forest and the wild;
My breast her shield in wintry weather,
And when the friendly sunshine smiled
And she would mark the opening skies,
I saw no Heaven but in her eyes —
Even childhood knows the human heart;
For when, in sunshine and in smiles,
From all our little cares apart,
Laughing at her half silly wiles,
I'd throw me on her throbbing breast,
And pour my spirit out in tears,
She'd look up in my wilder'd eye —
There was no need to speak the rest —
No need to quiet her kind fears —
She did not ask the reason why.
The hallow'd memory of those years
Comes o'er me in these lonely hours,
And, with sweet loveliness, appears
As perfume of strange summer flowers;
Of flowers which we have known before
In infancy, which seen, recall
To mind — not flowers alone — but more,
Our earthly life, and love — and all.

## VIII.

Yes! she was worthy of all love!
Even such as from the accursed time
My spirit with the tempest strove,

When on the mountain peak alone,
Ambition lent it a new tone,
And bade it first to dream of crime,
My frenzy to her bosom taught:
We still were young: no purer thought
Dwelt in a seraph's breast than *thine*;
For passionate love is still divine:
*I* loved her as an angel might
With ray of the all living light
Which blazes upon Edis' shrine.
It is not surely sin to name,
With such as mine — that mystic flame,
I had no being but in thee!
The world with all its train of bright
And happy beauty (for to me
All was an undefined delight),
The world — its joy — its share of pain
Which I felt not — its bodied forms
Of varied being, which contain
The bodiless spirits of the storms,
The sunshine, and the calm — the ideal
And fleeting vanities of dreams,
Fearfully beautiful! the real
Nothings of mid-day waking life —
Of an enchanted life, which seems,
Now as I look back, the strife
Of some ill demon, with a power
Which left me in an evil hour,
All that I felt, or saw, or thought,
Crowding, confused became

(With thine unearthly beauty fraught)
Thou — and the nothing of a name.

## IX.

The passionate spirit which hath known,
And deeply felt the silent tone
Of its own self supremacy, —
(I speak thus openly to thee,
'Twere folly *now* to veil a thought
With which this aching breast is fraught)
The soul which feels its innate right —
The mystic empire and high power
Given by the energetic might
Of Genius, at its natal hour;
Which knows (believe me at this time,
When falsehood were a tenfold crime,
There *is* a power in the high spirit
To *know* the fate it will inherit)
The soul, which knows such power, will still
Find *Pride* the ruler of its will.
Yes! I was proud — and ye who know
The magic of that meaning word,
So oft perverted, will bestow
Your scorn, perhaps, when ye have heard
That the proud spirit had been broken,
The proud heart burst in agony
At one upbraiding word or token
Of her that heart's idolatry —
I was ambitious — have ye known

Its fiery passion? — ye have not —
A cottager, I mark'd a throne
Of half the world, as all my own,
And murmur'd at such lowly lot!
But it had pass'd me as a dream
Which, of light step, flies with the dew,
That kindling thought — did not the beam
Of Beauty, which did guide it through
The livelong summer day, oppress
My mind with double loveliness —

## X.

We walk'd together on the crown
Of a high mountain, which look'd down
Afar from its proud natural towers
Of rock and forest, on the hills —
The dwindled hills, whence amid bowers
Her own fair hand had rear'd around,
Gush'd shoutingly a thousand rills,
Which as it were, in fairy bound
Embraced two hamlets — those our own —
Peacefully happy — yet alone —
I spoke to her of power and pride —
But mystically, in such guise,
That she might deem it nought beside
The moment's converse; in her eyes
I read (perhaps too carelessly)
A mingled feeling with my own;
The flush on her bright cheek, to me,

Seem'd to become a queenly throne
Too well, that I should let it be
A light in the dark wild, alone.

## XI.

There — in that hour — a thought came o'er
My mind, it had not known before —
To leave her while we both were young, —
To follow my high fate among
The strife of nations, and redeem
The idle words, which, as a dream
Now sounded to her heedless ear —
I held no doubt — I knew no fear
Of peril in my wild career;
To gain an empire, and throw down
As nuptial dowry — a queen's crown,
The only feeling which possest,
With her own image, my fond breast —
Who, that had known the secret thought
Of a young peasant's bosom then,
Had deem'd him, in compassion, aught
But one, whom fantasy had led
Astray from reason — Among men
Ambition is chain'd down — nor fed
(As in the desert, where the grand,
The wild, the beautiful, conspire
With their own breath to fan its fire)
With thoughts such feeling can command;
Uncheck'd by sarcasm, and scorn

Of those, who hardly will conceive
That any should become "great," born
In their own sphere — will not believe
That they shall stoop in life to one
Whom daily they are wont to see
Familiarly — whom Fortune's sun
Hath ne'er shone dazzlingly upon,
Lowly — and of their own degree —

## XII.

I pictured to my fancy's eye
Her silent, deep astonishment,
When, a few fleeting years gone by,
(For short the time my high hope lent
To its most desperate intent,)
She might recall in him, whom Fame
Had gilded with a conqueror's name,
(With glory — such as might inspire
Perforce, a passing thought of one,
Whom she had deemed in his own fire
Withered and blasted; who had gone
A traitor, violate of the truth
So plighted in his early youth,)
Her own Alexis, who should plight
The love he plighted *then* — again.
And raise his infancy's delight.
The bride and queen of Tamerlane. —

## XIII.

One noon of a bright summer's day
I pass'd from out the matted bower
Where in a deep, still slumber lay
My Ada. In that peaceful hour,
A silent gaze was my farewell.
I had no other solace — then
To awake her, and a falsehood tell
Of a feign'd journey, were again
To trust the weakness of my heart
To her soft thrilling voice: To part
Thus, haply, while in sleep she dream'd
Of long delight, nor yet had deem'd
Awake, that I had held a thought
Of parting, were with madness fraught;
I knew not woman's heart, alas!
Tho' loved, and loving — let it pass. —

## XIV.

I went from out the matted bower,
And hurried madly on my way:
And felt, with every flying hour,
That bore me from my home, more gay;
There is of earth an agony
Which, ideal, still may be
The worst ill of mortality.
'Tis bliss, in its own reality,

Too real, to *his* breast who lives
Not within himself but gives
A portion of his willing soul
To God, and to the great whole —
To him, whose loving spirit will dwell
With Nature, in her wild paths; tell
Of her wondrous ways, and telling bless
Her overpowering loveliness!
A more than agony to him
Whose failing sight will grow dim
With its own living gaze upon
That loveliness around: the sun —
The blue sky — the misty light
Of the pale cloud therein, whose hue
Is grace to its heavenly bed of blue;
Dim! tho' looking on all bright!
O God! when the thoughts that may not pass
Will burst upon him, and alas!
For the flight on Earth to Fancy given,
There are no words — unless of Heaven.

## XV.

Look round thee now on Samarcand,
Is she not queen of earth? her pride
Above all cities? in her hand
Their destinies? with all beside
Of glory, which the world hath known?
Stands she not proudly and alone?
And who her sovereign? Timur, he

Whom the astonish'd earth hath seen,
With victory, on victory,
Redoubling age! and more, I ween,
The Zinghis' yet re-echoing fame.
And now what has he? what! a name.
The sound of revelry by night
Comes o'er me, with the mingled voice
Of many with a breast as light,
As if 'twere not the dying hour
Of one, in whom they did rejoice —
As in a leader, haply — Power
Its venom secretly imparts;
Nothing have I with human hearts.

## XVI.

When Fortune mark'd me for her own,
And my proud hopes had reach'd a throne
(It boots me not, good friar, to tell
A tale the world but knows too well,
How by what hidden deeds of might,
I clamber'd to the tottering height,)
I still was young; and well I ween
My spirit what it e'er had been.
My eyes were still on pomp and power,
My wilder'd heart was far away
In valleys of the wild Taglay,
In mine own Ada's matted bower.
I dwelt not long in Samarcand
Ere, in a peasant's lowly guise,
I sought my long-abandon'd land;
By sunset did its mountains rise
In dusky grandeur to my eyes:
But as I wander'd on the way
My heart sunk with the sun's ray.
To him, who still would gaze upon
The glory of the summer sun,
There comes, when that sun will from him part,
A sullen hopelessness of heart.
That soul will hate the evening mist
So often lovely, and will list
To the sound of the coming darkness (known
To those whose spirits hearken) as one
Who in a dream of night *would* fly,

But cannot, from a danger nigh.
What though the moon — the silvery moon —
Shine on his path, in her high noon;
*Her* smile is chilly, and *her* beam
In that time of dreariness will seem
As the portrait of one after death;
A likeness taken when the breath
Of young life, and the fire o' the eye,
*Had* lately been, but had pass'd by.
'Tis thus when the lovely summer sun
Of our boyhood, his course hath run:
For all we live to know — is known;
And all we seek to keep — hath flown;
With the noon-day beauty, which is all.
Let life, then, as the day-flower, fall —
The transient, passionate day-flower,()
Withering at the evening hour.

## XVII.

I reach'd my home — my home no more —
For all was flown that made it so —
I pass'd from out its mossy door,
In vacant idleness of woe.
There met me on its threshold stone
A mountain hunter, I had known
In childhood, but he knew me not.
Something he spoke of the old cot:
It had seen better days, he said;
*There* rose a fountain once, and *there*

Full many a fair flower raised its head:
But she who rear'd them was long dead,
And in such follies had no part,
What was there left me *now?* despair —
A kingdom for a broken — heart.

# FUGITIVE PIECES

I SAW thee on the bridal day,
When a burning blush came o'er thee,
Tho' Happiness around thee lay,
The world all love before thee.
And, in thine eye, the kindling light
Of young passion free
Was all on earth, my chained sight
Of Loveliness might see.
That blush, I ween, was maiden shame;
As such it well may pass:
Tho' its glow hath raised a fiercer flame
In the breast of him, alas!
Who saw thee on that bridal day.
When that deep blush *would* come o'er thee,
Tho' Happiness around thee lay;
The world all Love before thee. —

# DREAMS

OH! that my young life were a lasting dream!
My spirit not awakening, till the beam
Of an Eternity should bring the morrow.
Yes! tho' that long dream were of hopeless sorrow,
'Twere better than the cold reality
Of waking life, to him whose heart must be,
And hath been still, upon the lovely earth,
A chaos of deep passion, from his birth.
But should it be — that dream eternally
Continuing — as dreams have been to me
In my young boyhood — should it thus be given,
'Twere folly still to hope for higher Heaven.
For I have revell'd when the sun was bright
I' the summer sky, in dreams of living light,
And loveliness, — have left my very heart
In climes of mine imagining, apart
From mine own home, with beings that have been
Of mine own thought — what more could I have seen?
'Twas once — and only once — and the wild hour
From my remembrance shall not pass — some power
Or spell had bound me — 'twas the chilly wind
Came o'er me in the night, and left behind
Its image on my spirit — or the moon
Shone on my slumbers in her lofty noon

Too coldly — or the stars — howe'er it was
That dream was as that night-wind — let it pass.

I *have been* happy, tho' [but] in a dream.
I have been happy — and I love the theme:
Dreams! in their vivid colouring of life
As in that fleeting, shadowy, misty strife
Of semblance with reality which brings
To the delirious eye, more lovely things
Of Paradise and Love — and all our own!
Than young Hope in his sunniest hour hath known.

# VISIT OF THE DEAD

THY soul shall find itself alone —
Alone of all on earth — unknown
The cause — but none are near to pry
Into thine hour of secrecy.
Be silent in that solitude,
Which is not loneliness — for then
The spirits of the dead, who stood
In life before thee, are again
In death around thee, and their will
Shall then o'ershadow thee — be still:
For the night, tho' clear, shall frown;
And the stars shall look not down
From their thrones, in the dark heaven,
With light like Hope to mortals given.
But their red orbs, without beam,
To thy withering heart shall seem
As a burning, and a fever
Which would cling to thee for ever.
But 'twill leave thee, as each star
In the morning light afar
Will fly thee — and vanish:
— But its *thought* thou canst not banish.
The breath of God will be still;
And the mist upon the hill
By that summer breeze unbroken

Shall charm thee — as a token,
And a symbol which shall be
Secrecy in thee.

# EVENING STAR

'TWAS noontide of summer,
 And midtime of night,
And stars, in their orbits,
 Shone pale, through the light
Of the brighter, cold moon.
 'Mid planets her slaves,
Herself in the Heavens,
 Her beam on the waves.
 I gazed awhile
 On her cold smile;
Too cold-too cold for me —
 There passed, as a shroud,
 A fleecy cloud,
And I turned away to thee,
  Proud Evening Star,
 In thy glory afar
And dearer thy beam shall be;
 For joy to my heart
 Is the proud part
Thou bearest in Heaven at night.,
 And more I admire
 Thy distant fire,
Than that colder, lowly light.

# IMITATION

A DARK unfathom'd tide
Of interminable pride —
A mystery, and a dream,
Should my early life seem;
I say that dream was fraught
With a wild, and waking thought
Of beings that have been,
Which my spirit hath not seen,
Had I let them pass me by,
With a dreaming eye!
Let none of earth inherit
That vision on my spirit;
Those thoughts I would control,
As a spell upon his soul:
For that bright hope at last
And that light time have past.
And my worldly rest hath gone
With a sigh as it pass'd on:
I care not tho' it perish
With a thought I then did cherish.

# COMMUNION WITH NATURE

*How often we forget all time, when loneAdmiring Nature's universal throne;Her woods — her wilds — her mountains-the intenseReply of Hers to Our intelligence!*

*Byron*

## I

IN youth I have known one with whom the Earth
In secret communing held-as he with it,
In daylight, and in beauty, from his birth:
Whose fervid, flickering torch of life was lit
From the sun and stars, whence he had drawn forth
A passionate light such for his spirit was fit
And yet that spirit knew-not in the hour
Of its own fervor-what had o'er it power.

## II

Perhaps it may be that my mind is wrought
To a fever* by the moonbeam that hangs o'er,
But I will half believe that wild light fraught
With more of sovereignty than ancient lore

Hath ever told-or is it of a thought
The unembodied essence, and no more
That with a quickening spell doth o'er us pass
As dew of the night-time, o'er the summer grass?

## III

Doth o'er us pass, when, as th' expanding eye
To the loved object-so the tear to the lid
Will start, which lately slept in apathy?
And yet it need not be — (that object) hid
From us in life-but common-which doth lie
Each hour before us — but then only bid
With a strange sound, as of a harp-string broken
T' awake us — 'Tis a symbol and a token

## IV

Of what in other worlds shall be — and given
In beauty by our God, to those alone
Who otherwise would fall from life and Heaven
Drawn by their heart's passion, and that tone,
That high tone of the spirit which hath striven
Though not with Faith-with godliness — whose throne
With desperate energy 't hath beaten down;
Wearing its own deep feeling as a crown.

# A WILDER'D BEING FROM MY BIRTH

A WILDER'D being from my birth,
My spirit spurn'd control,
But now, abroad on the wide earth.
Where wanderest thou, my soul?
In visions of the dark night
I have dream'd of joy departed —
But a waking dream of life and light
Hath left me broken-hearted.
And what is not a dream by day
To him whose eyes are cast
On things around him with a ray
Turn'd back upon the past?
That holy dream — that holy dream,
While all the world were chiding,
Hath cheered me as a lovely beam
A lonely spirit guiding —
What tho' that light, thro' misty night
So dimly shone afar —
"What could there be more purely bright
In Truth's day-star?

# THE HAPPIEST DAY — THE HAPPIEST HOUR

THE happiest day — the happiest hour
My sear'd and blighted heart hath known,
The highest hope of pride and power,
I feel hath flown.
Of power! said I? yes! such I ween;
But they have vanished long, alas!
The visions of my youth have been —
But let them pass.
And, pride, what have I now with thee?
Another brow may even inherit
The venom thou hast pour'd on me —
Be still, my spirit.
The happiest day — the happiest hour
Mine eyes shall see — have ever seen,
The brightest glance of pride and power,
I feel — have been:
But were that hope of pride and power
Now offer'd, with the pain
Even *then* I felt — that brightest hour
I would not live again:
For on its wing was dark alloy.
And as it flutter'd — fell

An essence — powerful to destroy
A soul that knew it well.

# THE LAKE

IN spring of youth it was my lot
To haunt of the wide earth a spot
The which I could not love the less —
So lovely was the loneliness
Of a wild lake, with black rock bound,
And the tall pines that tower'd around.
But when the Night had thrown her pall
Upon that spot, as upon all,
And the mystic wind went by
Murmuring in melody —
Then — ah then I would awake
To the terror of the lone lake.
Yet that terror was not fright,
But a tremulous delight —
A feeling not the jewelled mine
Could teach or bribe me to define —
Nor Love — although the Love were thine.
Death was in that poisonous wave,
And in its gulf a fitting grave
For him who thence could solace bring
To his lone imagining —
Whose solitary soul could make
An Eden of that dim lake.